Hidden Hippo

For my son Geoff, who shared part of this adventure, and for
my grandchildren, Gregory and Alyssa — J. G.

For Amelia — C. B.

With special thanks from the author to Maartje van Westerop and Peter Westerveld for
making her first safari in Kenya possible, Frans J. Engelsma, retired zoo biologist,
for his expertise and patience, and Bryna Hellman for her wisdom and wit.

First published in Great Britain in 2008 by Barefoot Books, Ltd
This paperback edition published in 2011

This book has been printed on 100% acid-free paper
Graphic design by Barefoot Books, Bath
Colour reproduction by B & P International, Hong Kong
Printed and bound in China by Printplus, Ltd

This book was typeset in Grilled Cheese Condensed and Plantin Schoolbook
The illustrations were prepared in antique fabrics
and felt with buttons, beads and assorted bric-a-brac
ISBN 978-1-84686-532-9

British Cataloguing-in-Publication Data: a catalogue record
for this book is available from the British Library

1 3 5 7 9 8 6 4 2

Hidden Hippo

Written by Joan Gannij

Illustrated by Clare Beaton

Barefoot Books
Celebrating Art and Story

When I went exploring,
I wanted to see
A hippo or two,
Perhaps even three?

I saw cheetahs and rhinos,
I gave them a wink.
By the lake were flamingos
In bright shades of pink.

I saw lots of lions,
I saw chimpanzees.

I spotted some leopards
Relaxing in trees.

Zebras and wildebeests
Headed downstream.

Enormous grey elephants
Splashed themselves clean!

Giraffes glided by
So graceful and tall,
Followed by dik-diks
So quick and so small.

On the shore of the river
Down in the glade,
Crocodile families
Slept in the shade.

But something was missing —
Oh, where could it be?

I couldn't stop searching.
I just had to see.

Then to my surprise,
I heard a loud splash.
And there was a hippo —
As quick as a flash!

My journey has ended,
But I won't forget
Those well-hidden hippos
I finally met.

Animals of the African Plains

African elephants are the largest land animals.
They are slightly bigger than Asian elephants and
have larger, less rounded ears. Elephants use their
trunks for smelling, breathing, trumpeting, drinking,
and for grabbing things to eat, such as leaves,
branches, roots, grasses, fruits and bark.

Cheetahs are the world's fastest land animal. They
can run as fast as 70 miles per hour and when they
run, it looks as if only one foot at a time is touching
the ground. They need bushes, tall grass and other
large plants to hide from predators.

Chimpanzees are our closest living relatives. These
social creatures normally walk on all fours, which is
called 'knuckle walking', but they can also stand
and walk upright. They spend most of their time in
the woods, where you can see them swinging from
branch to branch in the trees.

Crocodiles have been around since the age of dinosaurs, between 65 and 135 million years ago. The most common is the Nile crocodile, which can grow to up to 16 feet (4.8 metres) in length! The crocodile is the hippo's main enemy.

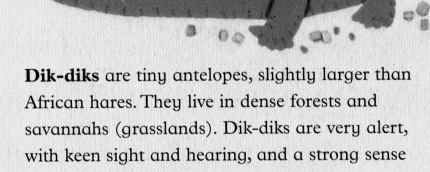

Dik-diks are tiny antelopes, slightly larger than African hares. They live in dense forests and savannahs (grasslands). Dik-diks are very alert, with keen sight and hearing, and a strong sense of smell.

Giraffes are the world's tallest land animal. Their long legs allow them to run as fast as 35 miles per hour. Their distinctive skin patterns differ from one type of giraffe to another. Giraffes love to eat the leaves of acacia trees, which they have no trouble reaching because of their long necks.

Greater flamingos are the most widespread species of flamingo, found in Asia and southern Europe as well as Africa. They live in large groups called colonies and usually gather together in shallow lakes. Their diet includes algae, which gives them their bright shades of pink. They also eat small fish and shrimp.

Leopards are usually light in colour with distinctive dark spots, but there are also black leopards known as 'black panthers'. Graceful and powerful, leopards are solitary creatures that are primarily nocturnal. During the day, when not hunting, you can see them resting in trees or in thick bush.

Lions are the only cats that live in groups, called prides. Although the females do the hunting, it is the males who defend the territory, by roaring or chasing away intruders. Only male lions have manes.

Rhinos are divided into five species, two African and three Asian. The two African species are the white rhino and the black rhino, both of which have two horns. Rhinos are herbivores, which means they only eat plants. Like the hippo, they have massive bodies and stumpy legs. The rhinoceros is one of the most endangered species in the world.

Wildebeests, also known as gnus, are a kind of large antelope. Every February, over a million wildebeests make the annual migration of more than 800 miles from the Serengeti north through open woodlands, plains and rivers to feed on the grasslands in the Masai Mara. They migrate during the dry season following the seasonal rains. They usually complete their circular journey and return home by November.

Zebras graze together in herds, primarily on grass. They have excellent hearing and eyesight and can run at speeds of up to 35 miles per hour. They clean themselves by taking dust baths! Zebras also join the wildebeests on their migration, along with Thomson's gazelles.

Endangered Species

The wildlife and people of Africa have lived together in relative harmony for thousands of years. It was only in the twentieth century that things began to change dramatically. Wildlife started to feel the pressure from the effects of human activities, which have damaged their habitats and spread disease. Many African animals have also been overhunted.

In recent decades, conservation efforts have been initiated by wildlife organisations to save the groups of animals which are seriously in danger of becoming extinct: from elephants and rhinos, to zebras, chimpanzees and mountain gorillas, among others. Various measures have been introduced, such as banning the ivory trade, regulating hunting and creating rhino sanctuaries.

Ecotourism projects have reduced the pressure on nomadic farmers to have more and more livestock. Economic incentives have been developed for local communities to encourage the planting of trees. These are just a few of the constructive options for enabling Africa's great animals and local peoples to live together peacefully. Please contact the following organisations to find out how you can help:

World Wildlife Fund www.wwf.org.uk
East African Wildlife Society www.eawildlife.org
International Fund for Animal Welfare www.ifaw.org

Meet the Hippo!

The hippopotamus is the third largest mammal on land, after the elephant and the rhinoceros. It can weigh half a ton, about 1,000 pounds (455 kilos) or more, while the average lifespan of a hippo in the wild is 20–30 years. Hippos have excellent sight and hearing, as well as an acute sense of smell. The hippo can run quite fast, about 18 miles per hour, and can turn quickly and climb steep banks.

Hippos actually spend more time in water than on land, a total of 18–20 hours a day! When they are underwater, they appear to dance or walk in graceful slow motion by springing from the bottom, which can be quite comical. Hippos need water or mud to keep cool as they do not have sweat glands.

At night, hippos emerge from the water to graze on wild grass or plants. They often walk up to five miles in search of the best spot. They spend part of their day digesting, socialising, and sleeping in the shade, then re-enter the water to cool off and rest. Although hippos look cute and cuddly, they are one of the most dangerous animals in Africa, with only lions and crocodiles as their primary enemies.